A THOUSAND PARALLEL LIVES

A THOUSAND PARALLEL LIVES

Tenzin Pema Chashar

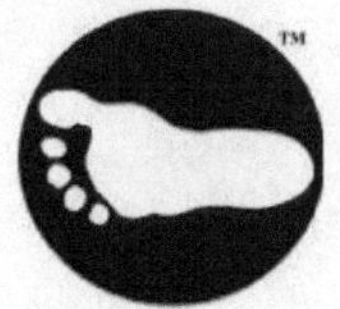

Bigfoot Publications
Because, there's a writer in everyone.

A Thousand Parallel Lives
Author: Tenzin Pema Chashar

First Published by
Bigfoot06 Publications (OPC) Pvt. Ltd.
B-10,12 Shree Shyam Palace,
Sector 4,5 Chowk, Old Railway Road,
Gurugram, Haryana (122001)
Website: www.bigfootpublications.in
Email: info@bigfootpublications.in

First Edition : April, 2023
©Tenzin Pema Chashar

ISBN Print Book - **978-81-19201-11-2**

Printed in India

Dedication
In honor of the Sun and Moon of the Tibetan World

PREFACE

"You will leave everything you love most: this is the arrow that the bow of exile shoots first. You will know how salty another's bread tastes and how hard it is to ascend and descend another's stairs."

– Dante

ACKNOWLEDGMENT

Forever grateful to my beloved Amala - Dickey Dolma, my late Pala - Tsering Thupten Chashar, and late Agula - Dhamchoe Yarphel Chashar, who painted the very first pictures of home and early exile life in my mind through their vivid storytelling and impassioned efforts to instill a strong sense of Tibetan identity in me through everything they did and said.

I remain indebted also to the many elders in the Tibetan diaspora who have strived so hard to preserve and promote our unique cultural and religious identity, building a rock-solid foundation that has enabled the younger Tibetan generation to thrive in different villages, towns, cities, and countries across the world.

My sincere gratitude also to my dear Ama Chungla, the families of my sister Tenzing Zompa and brother Sonam Gyatso, Venerable Khenpo Ngedhon Tenzin Rinpoche, Venerable Lobsang Dorjee Gapak, my many loving family members of the families of Chari Sharma, Wangden Deyram, Trompa Khangsar, and Mendong, and so many of my dearest friends of many decades for being among my most vocal and steadfast champions.

And finally, only love and untold gratitude for Jigme Dorjee, my partner, pillar of strength, and biggest cheerleader of everything I do, including this book of poems, and for my three children – Tara Kesang, Tenzin Kunkyi, and Tenzin Mipham Namgyal – who inspire me everyday to try to be a better human being and to strive to leave a positive imprint in this world, albeit a small one.

CONTENTS

******

A Thousand Parallel Lives

In the dark of the night, under a blanket of stars,
A timid little girl crouched down on the ground,
Her eyes forever up, searching for patterns in the sky,
Her ears taking in the sounds of a village asleep,
Her lips mouthing a song, the lyrics carefully mastered,
Over many stolen moments, between study time and play.

She went about her business,
with an unhurried pace,
As her father stood guard,
out of sight yet within earshot,
"My child, when you go for the party tomorrow,
The other girls your age will sway with finesse to every tune,
But you, my child, can you dance if you need to,
or learn a move or two, To fit in with the others,
because you will need to," he said.

"O Father," the little girl said, "Worry not."
"I know a step or two, as well as to act as if I do,
So I'll have no trouble fitting in or seeming like one of them,
But that too, only if I want to."
And her father smiled to himself in the dark,
While waiting patiently for the girl,
As he pondered that answer and all its weight,
The fearlessness, the confidence, and the innocence.

******

At the crack of dawn, under a fluorescent tube light,
An unsure young bride hunched over her kitchen table,
Her hands forever moving – creating and then repairing,
Her eyes sizing each log of wood, every handful of corn cob,
Her mind racing through the same list of tasks – imperative yet insignificant,
To be toiled through days and weeks and months on end, until winter comes.

She boiled the water over the fire, as she hastened to finish her other chores,
Her thoughts turning to the words of her sister, uttered in the kitchen of her mother's home;
"My sister, when you go to your husband's home tomorrow,
The hands of the other young brides your age will be marked by calluses and corns, While you,
my sister, with your soft and gentle hands, will you be as able as them,
And fit in with the other brides your age, because you will need to," she said.

"O Sister," the young bride recalls saying, "Worry not."
"I know how to churn butter and roast barley, as Mother oft did,
But better still, to bargain and make a sale when winter comes calling,
So I'll have no trouble fitting in or standing out, whichever I may choose." And her sister had smiled uneasily at her that morning,
Her face fraught with worry, searching for signs of reassurance, As she considered that answer and all its truths,
The precociousness, the uncertainty, and the optimism.

***

In the heat of the afternoon, under a dust-laden fan,
A matronly woman, middle-aged, poured over the contents of her suitcase,
Her hands weighing time and again, the things she had chosen to start afresh,
Her silent, timorous tears falling on carefully folded clothes,
Her heart laden with apprehension, overpowering her hopes
For what lay before her – the end of one life, the promise of another.

She hurried through her packing, a charm box and a *peja*[1] atop a heap of documents,
While her husband waited in the shadows, as if readying for the long wait ahead;
"My wife, when you go to this foreign land tomorrow,
The people of your new home will expect, that you talk and eat and walk like them,
But you, my wife, will you learn a language that you haven't heard or live like you're one of them,
In a desperate bid to fit in, because you will need to," he said.

"O Husband," the woman said, "Worry not."
"I know a sentence or two, or to replace a missing word with a kind smile or deed,
To trust the blood of our elders that course through our veins, their steely determination and fortitude,
It'll enable me, I'm sure, to rebuild and belong; to experience the best of both worlds."
And her husband smiled gratefully at her that afternoon,
As he helped her prepare the things that would define the foundations of a new life,
All the while reflecting on her answer and all its truths,
The perseverance, the courage, and the hope.

***

---

[1]* *Peja: Tibetan scriptures and prayer books*

Aashia Gough
PHOTOGRAPHER

At the fag end of a long day, under the light of the setting sun,
A wise old lady sat in her blue armchair,
Her eyes forever darting, from one flower bed to the next in her gently loved garden,
Her right hand turning a prayer wheel, her left a rosary with 108 prayer beads,
Her lips chanting a prayer – words, paragraphs and whole pages from memory,
Etched forever in all corners of her mind, ready to be wielded at any waking moment.

She went about her evening, with an unhurried pace; watching,
As her grandson wandered about – always within sight, always with a question;
"My Grandmother, when you go for the teachings tomorrow,
The other elders your age, will soak in every syllable of the Dharma,
But you, my *MomoLa*[2*], with your many years away from it all, will you understand,
And know what to chant and when and why, because you will need to," he said.

"O Grandson," the old lady said, "Worry not."
"I know enough about the Dharma, or as much as I should,
To chant in unison with the others in the congregation, or to stop, to listen, to be,
But never to fit in; no, never that; only to be who I truly am, only to just be."
And her grandson smiled softly as the sun moved beyond the horizon,
Bending his head forward towards his grandmother, foreheads touching,
While the old lady hoped he had comprehended her answer and all its wisdom,
The resilience, the defiance, and the poise.

[2*] *MomoLa: Grandmother*

The Sun and Moon

The Sun and Moon rise,
A thousand precious lifetimes,
For the red-faced race.

The Sun and Moon shine,
Their light brighter, dearer,
As the dragon circles.

The Sun and Moon beam,
Across seas, mountains, desserts,
Breathing life, anew.

The Sun and Moon see,
The waiting, su"ering, strife,
Succumbing to fate.

The Sun and Moon pray,
A thousand o"erings made,
For unity, emptiness.

The Sun and Moon wait,
Like the roof of the world,
their Glorious return.

The Sacrifice of Love

My child,
Ask not of me,
Why you had to leave,
Why I had to stay,
For your questions I hear every waking hour;
Ask instead,
What it means to love so unconditionally,
Ask instead,
What it means to make the sacrifice of love.

My child,
Weep not for me,
When you think of me,
For your tears I see in the Holy Lake,
Each time I go there searching
For signs of your well-being.

My child,
Worry not for me,
When you read the news,
For your anxiety and disquiet awaken me,
Each time I close my eyes to dream
To relive our life together,
A life interrupted.

My child,
Call not for me,
When you long to speak,
For your cries silence mine and all who remain,
Each time wearing us down or wiping us away,
Always, a tad bit more than the last time,
Until nothing remains.

My child,
Ask not of me,
Why you had to leave,
Why I had to stay,
For your questions I hear every waking hour;
Ask instead,
What it means to love so unconditionally,
Ask instead,
What it means to make the sacrifice of love.

***

Ode to the Red Palace

The Potala stands
Majestic. Resilient.
Just like its people.

My Beloved Amala

My beloved *Amala*[3],
Many seasons and many moons have passed,
Since we said our goodbyes,
You to stay and me to leave,
For reasons far beyond the comprehension
Of my then seven-year-old mind.

My beloved Amala,
In the kitchen of my new home,
I go, each time, near the fire,
To boil tea or cook a meal,
But mostly, I go so my clothes will carry
The scent of smoke; the scent of you.

---

[3] *Amala: Means 'Honorable Mother' in Tibetan*

My beloved Amala,
In the tiny shop of my new school,
Where the other children go to spend
The hard-earned coins of their parents;
There, I go each day, to see the jar of sugar candies -
The kind that reminds me only of your generous smile.

My beloved Amala,
At the end of each long day,
When most long to rest their minds,
I prefer, instead, to gaze up at the sky,
The setting sun evoking memories of you,
Prompting quiet tears that are as deafening as your absence.

My beloved Amala,
Many years and many decades have passed,
Since we said our goodbyes,
You to stay and me to leave,
For reasons still beyond the comprehension
Of my now seventy-year-old mind.

The Call to Arms

Listen carefully
And you will hear,
The call to arms –
So fierce, so sure,
So brazen, so bold;
No hint of doubt,
Nor trace of fear.
Come learn, they said.
Learn the drill.
To prepare ourselves for what is to come.

The calls, unrelenting,
Come every morning,
Prompting the young – the men and women,
To gather each day,
Their wooden toy guns blazing,
In the village school yard,
Surrounded by acres of corn fields,
And the conspiracy of the ravens,
Perched atop rows of Eucalyptus trees.

And so they stood, shoulder to shoulder,
Marching - Left, Right, Left; Left, Right, Left;
Their collective enthusiasm shrouding
The lack of harmony
In the movement of their feet,
Even as the leader shouted out the orders,
Willing them to work in unison,
Whether to move forward or to stop,
To stand at ease or at attention.

Soon it became a ritual,
Another addition to their morning chores,
As the young - the men and women,
Slinging their guns on their shoulders,
Heeded, each day, the call to arms,
Readying to fight a war, they said, is coming,
Unannounced and sudden, in terrains unknown.
But prepare we can, they said. Prepare we must.
As they gathered each day for their daily drill.

The Stone Bench

Alone it stood, at the center of two neighborly homes,
The rustic stone bench;
Where many a good friend gathered each evening,
Reminiscing, remembering, recalling, repeating
Every little memory – fresh or fading,
Of home and hearth, family and friends,
Of hurried departures and narrow escapes,
Of serendipitous reunions and of rebuilding,
Of new homes purposefully built amongst those with a shared past.

And so it quietly stood, a silent member of this daily party,
The old weathered stone bench;
Where the others came each day, as if to gather for a ritual,
Discussing, dissecting, deliberating, debating
Every tiny detail of a life – relived or relieved,
Of the whitewash of houses against the maroon of the monasteries,
Of ravens, barley fields, yaks, and horses – as far as the eye can see,
Of the scent of their mother's apron and of fresh butter,
Of the taste of sweet, butterless tea, and the sight of blazing corn fields.

Rigid and invincible it stood, the keeper of many truths,
The rugged stone bench;
Where the crevices of its ragged, rough edges, each house a story,
Unforgettable, unprecedented, unearthly, untold;
Every turn of events in a tale – familiar yet unique,
Of divine interventions and oracles, omens and miracles,
Of bellowing, clamoring, and shouting in alien alleyways,
Of many moons spent thriving in the prison walls of a free country,
Of practicing for wars with wooden toy guns, but fighting it, always,
with compassion.

The Gift of the Goddess

Thousands of praises,
Beseech the Goddess; Heeding,
A child, she bestows.

The Scorpion

The scorpion swims,
In a wok of boiling hot oil,
Its pincers and tail soaking up
All evils of the past,
All obstacles of the present,
All possible hurdles of the future,
Just before *Losar*[4]* comes.

The scorpion waits,
For the other dough-shaped *Khabsays*[5]*,
To do their time in the scalding oil,
The *Bhungu Amchoks*[6]* in all their glory,
The Bulug, the pimbi-tok-tok, the mukdung, and the nyapsha,
The hrug-hrugs and their more elite designer siblings,
In preparation for the new year.

The scorpion hangs,
Above the stove of every Tibetan's kitchen,
Forever suspended with a *Katag*[7]* around its waist,
A silent judge of every meal cooked,
A witness to every conversation exchanged,
A collector of every form of grease and dust,
All through the year, from the very first day of Losar.

---

[4]* *Losar: Means Tibetan New Year*

[5]* *Khabsays: Literally translates to 'Mouth-eat,' these are fried Tibetan flour-based cookies made during the New Year; the diff erent type of Khabsays include the Bhungu Amchok, Bulug, pimbi-tok-tok, mukdung, nyapsha, hrug-hrugs, specially designed cookies molded using food color, sanga bhaglep, tseytang kotsey, and more*

[6]* *Bhungu Amchoks: Literally translates to 'Donkey's ears.' These are fried Tibetan flour-based cookies molded in the shape of large Donkey's ears and take pride of place in the Losar altar off erings*

[7]* *Katag: Tibetan ceremonial silk white scarf*

Here vs. There

Tell me the sun shines,
As gently there as it does here.

Tell me the barley grows,
As abundantly there as it does here.

Tell me the butter tastes and looks,
As creamy and rich there as it does here.

Tell me the black-necked cranes descend and dance,
As majestically there as they do here.

Tell me the mustard fields glow,
As luminously like rows of gold as they do here.

Tell me the monastery towers gleam,
As fulgently from a distance as they do here.

Tell me the heart will feel,
As full and free there as it does here.

***

Quietly Waiting

Gracefully, ever so quietly, she moved.
Her hair in a hundred different plaits,
Her *Chuba*[8]* smoothed down
By the weight of carefully folded clothes.

Churning the butter tea in her *dongmo*[9]*,
Unhurriedly, she gazed out her window,
Only the worry lines on her calm face,
Revealing the many hours and days of waiting.

***

---

[8]* *Chuba: Tibetan traditional dress worn by the women and men*

[9]* *Dongmo: A tea-mixing cylinder used for churning butter and making Tibetan butter tea*

Our Friend, Hope

Hope – the powerful,
Unyielding, loyal friend of
Whole generations.

Lessons in Acceptance

Acceptance,
They teach us its power under a canopy of trees,
In the hallowed, opulent grounds of the brilliantly adorned monasteries.
Where men and women, old and young,
Sit fanning themselves and their children,
As the sweltering sun, unforgiving, burns their already tanned skin.

Acceptance,
They teach us its energy as the tea is being served,
In paper cups and enamel mugs and delicate little ceramic cups.
Amidst the frenzied confusion of young monks dashing about,
Carrying heavy aluminum tea kettles in the crowd,
Even as their eyes deftly find a lone empty cup that needs filling.

Acceptance,
They teach us its necessity as we await the consecrated offerings,
In paper napkins and wooden bowls and carefully preserved plastic bags.
While a sea of hands – some open, some pushing, some beckoning,
Wait impatiently for these tangible proofs of their devotion, Oblivious,
unheeding to the true gift the Gods had already bestowed.

O Yarlung Tsangpo

Gentle, graceful like
A ballerina you move,
O Yarlung Tsangpo.

The Young, the Holy, and the Wealthy

The message came one early morning,
It was the shepherd who heard it first,
They were coming for us, he said,
They are coming for the young, the holy, and the wealthy.

We cobbled together that morning,
Our shepherd recounting the details,
They had earmarked the houses and the places, he said,
Where the young, the holy, and the wealthy reside.

The sheep in the pens forgotten that morning,
As we speculated and strategized and organized,
For they have decreed, the shepherd said, to remove
From this earth, the young, the holy, and the wealthy.

The bags were hastily packed that evening,
The deities consulted, the offerings made,
To embark on the journey we must make,
With haste, before the morning comes.
For they are coming. They are coming.
They are coming for the young, the holy, and the wealthy.

Wait for Me

Please wait for me,
By the river beyond that mountain,
The halfway point to our destination;
I'll come when the time is ripe,
And together we shall cross the bigger mountains,
To the land where the people only wear white.

If the tsampa is running out,
Or the bag with the dried yak meat is thinning,
Don't despair. Just wait for me.
I'll come laden, with more bags of food,
To last us as we make our way across,
To the land where the people only wear white.

When the nights are cold, And the days run long,
Don't be afraid. Think of me.
For I'll be there, before the season turns,
So that together we may welcome the new season,
In the land where the people only wear white.

When your hope runs dry,
Or the prayers refuse to escape your cracked, bloody lips.
Don't give up. Hold out for me.
I'm around the corner.
Making my way to you.
So together we can soldier on and descend the mountains,
To the land where the people only wear white.

The Things I See

I see a mountain bedecked with wild flowers,
And in the grasslands below, the proud, stately creature you called your own.

I see the white-washed compound walls of your home,
And at its entrance, the two black majestic *Dok-Kyhi(s)*[10] that stood guard.

I see the grand prayer halls of the monastery,
And in its walls, the sea of maroon that ruled your world.

I see the holy lake before which you stood,
And in the water below, the prophecy you saw of the times to come.

I see the wrinkles on your tanned, brown skin,
And in your eyes, the yearning to walk the earth you call home.

***

---

[10]* *Dok-Kyhi(s): Tibetan mastiff or translated into nomad dog.*

The Songs of the Elders

They twirl like the wind,
Feets, hips, hands – obeying, the
Songs of the elders.

To Surrender to Emptiness

The familiar smell of burnt juniper leaves,
Wade through the halls,
Leaving white trails in its wake,
From the foot of the altar
In the *Choe-khang*[11*] —
The oasis of any Tibetan.

Inside, the gods and goddesses watch over the world,
From intricately hand-painted Thangkas,
From sturdy silver charm boxes, tarnished with age,
From gold-gilded regal statues,
Adorned with silk brocades and snow white katags[12*],
And hand-crafted necklaces of pearls, coral, and turquoise.

They gaze down at you as you make your offerings –
Of water, flowers, incense, light, perfume, food, music;
Some with peaceful expressions, others more wrathful,
The butter lamps illuminating their faces,
As if infusing life into the statues,
Willing them to assume human form.

We whisper our aspirations and fervently chant our prayers,
As the silver, copper and brass offering bowls,
Bear witness each day to our devotion and piety,
The comforting daily ritual an abiding reminder,
To release the shackles that bind us – desire, greed, selfishness;
To surrender, instead – wholly and completely – to the promise of
emptiness.

[11*] *Choe-khang: Literally translates to the prayer room in a Tibetan's home.*

[12*] *Katags: The ceremonial silk scarf, generally white in color.*

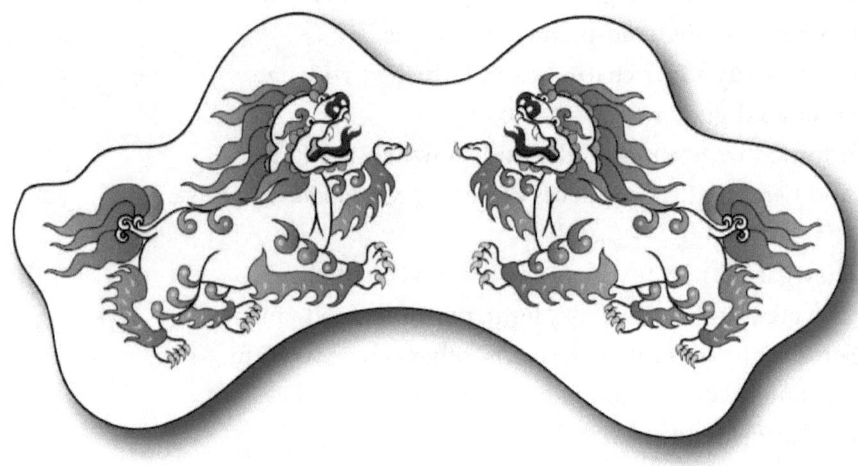

The Archer of the Poisoned Arrow

Fearless, selfless, bold,
The archer takes aim and shoots,
The poisoned arrow

Saved by the Precious One

The sound of the bullet,
Cracked through the wind,
Sharp, ear-piercing, deafening.
Its impact instant, knocking him down,
The sound of a thousand dreams shattering.

But he survived the journey, they said.
Survived the weeks-long treacherous escape across the mountains.
He survived because of the Precious One.

For the big silver charm box he wore around his waist,
It was there the bullet had lodged.
And he was saved, they said,
Saved by the power of his prayers,
And the strength of his beliefs,
Saved by the Precious One.

***

The sound of the bullet,
Cracked through the wind,
Sharp, ear-piercing, deafening.
Its impact instant, knocking him down,
The sound of a thousand dreams shattering.

But he survived the 1971 war, they said.
Survived the months-long fighting to liberate a country that
wasn't his. He survived because of the Precious One.

For the big silver charm box he wore around his waist,
It was there the bullet had lodged.
And he was saved, they said,
Saved by the power of his prayers,
And the strength of his beliefs,
Saved by the Precious One.

***

BIGFOOT PUBLICATIONS
Invite you to join us

Instagram

facebook